Mommy, Why Don't We Celebrate Halloween?

Linda Hacon Winwood

A Winwood Original

About the Logo

My daughter Sarah was born with six fingers on both hands and six toes on her left foot. When our children did artwork or sent homemade cards, we put a six-toed foot on the back of the cards like Hallmark puts a logo on theirs. That was the beginning of the Winwood logo.

Destiny Image® **Publishers, Inc.**
P.O. Box 310
Shippensburg, PA 17257-0310

"Speaking to the Purposes of God for This Generation
and for the Generations to Come"

ISBN 1-56043-823-1

For Worldwide Distribution
Printed in the U.S.A.

Third Printing: 1996   Fourth Printing: 1997

This book and all other Destiny Image, Revival Press, and Treasure House books are available at Christian bookstores and distributors worldwide.

For a U.S. bookstore nearest you, call **1-800-722-6774**.
For more information on foreign distributors, call **717-532-3040**.
Or reach us on the Internet: **http://www.reapernet.com**

Mommy, Why Don't We Celebrate Halloween?

Linda Hacon Winwood

This book is dedicated to my four beautiful children,
Amy, Sarah, Anna, and Katie,
and to all God's children who ask why.

My special thanks goes to a dear friend and sister in the Lord,
Sue Stevenson, for encouraging and supporting me,
and most of all for believing in me and this book.

"October 31st again and all the kids are trick-or-treating," said Jerry as he looked out the window in front of his house. "Mom, why can't we go trick-or-treating like all the other kids? Are you afraid we'll eat too much candy and our teeth will rot?"

"Well, Jerry," said Mom, "I certainly don't want your teeth to rot, but no, that isn't the reason you can't go trick-or-treating. As Christians, Daddy and I don't let you take part in Halloween because we know Jesus doesn't want us to do such things."

"But why, Mommy?" Sarah exclaimed. "What's wrong with Halloween?"

"Think for a moment, children, about other holidays we celebrate. Take Christmas, for example. How does Christmas make you feel?" asked Mom.

"Happy!" exclaimed Sarah.

"Excited," added Jerry.

"That's right," said Mom. "Christmas is a time of happiness and excitement as we celebrate the birth of Baby Jesus. Do you remember what the angel told the shepherds the night He was born?"

"Yes," said Sarah. "The angel told the shepherds good news of peace and great joy."

"That's right," said Mom. "Halloween has none of these. Halloween is filled with fear, meanness, and sadness."

"I don't understand, Mom," said Jerry. "How is dressing up in funny costumes and going door-to-door to get candy scary or sad?"

"The devil is very good at making things look wonderful on the outside that are wrong on the inside. Halloween is one of those things," Mom said.

"Many Christians haven't been taught the true meaning behind Halloween. They can't see the truth behind the costumes, parades, and candy of Halloween," continued Mom. "Only when we know the truth about something can we know whether it is good or bad for us. That's why the Bible says we are free when we know the truth."*

"So, what's the truth about Halloween, Mom?" Sarah asked. "Why shouldn't Christians take part in its fun?"

*   See John 8:32.

"Let me see if I can explain it a bit better," Mom said. "First, let's think about Christmas again. When the three wise men came to visit Baby Jesus, what did they bring Him?"

"Presents!" Sarah said.

"Yes, presents," Mom agreed. "When they gave Jesus the presents, the wise men knelt before Jesus to show that they honored Him."

"What does it mean to honor someone?" Jerry asked.

"To honor someone means that you show great respect for that person. You show that you understand his importance and great worth," Mom replied.

"But we don't kneel before anyone at Halloween," Sarah protested.

"You see, Sarah," Mom said, "there are many ways to show honor. One way is to set aside a special day, a holiday, to remember some important person or event."

"Yes!" Jerry agreed. "Thanksgiving reminds us of the big dinner the Pilgrims shared with the Indians to thank God for His help in the New World."

"Exactly," Mom responded. "What event do we celebrate at Easter?"

"That's when the angel rolled away the stone," Sarah answered. "Jesus wasn't dead anymore!"

"That's right," Mom replied. "At Easter we remember God's love when He sent Jesus to die on the cross for our sins. We also honor God for His great power that brought Jesus from death to life."

"So what do we honor at Halloween?" Jerry asked.

"A long time ago," Mom answered, "many people did not believe in God or honor His Son, Jesus. Instead they honored statues made of wood or stone. They also worshiped things in nature like the sun and the stars."

"Do you mean they bowed down to them like the wise men knelt before Baby Jesus?" Sarah asked.

"Yes, Sarah," Mom said. "They sang praises to their statues just like we sing praises to Jesus. They believed that the sun and stars had great power."

"God must not have liked that! He wants us to worship only Him," Jerry said.

"You are right, Jerry," Mom replied. "God's first laws for His people teach us not to worship any other gods or to bow down to their statues."*

"But, Mommy, we don't worship any statues or other gods at Halloween," Sarah said.

"In many parts of the world," Mom answered, "Halloween is a religious holiday—a holiday when people worship satan and honor evil. In fact, it is the biggest holiday on satan's calendar, kind of like Christmas and Easter on our calendar."

"But why?" Jerry asked. "Where's the evil in Halloween?"

*   See Exodus 20:3-5.

"Long ago the people who worshiped statues and nature also believed that the spirits of the dead could control the living," Mom said. "They thought that the souls of wicked people who had died returned on Halloween to harm or scare the living."

"That sounds dumb," said Jerry.

"These people didn't think so," Mom replied. "So they tried to keep the evil spirits happy by setting out sweets and other types of treats. They wanted the evil spirits to stay away and not trick them."

"Oh, I see," said Sarah, "and that's also where the trick-or-treat part of Halloween comes from."

"That's right," said Mom. "A group of farmers in Ireland, called Celts, asked everyone in the village to bring food to a town party. Then they gave the food to the evil spirits by burning it in a big bonfire. They even burned animals to feed the spirits.

"Many villagers wore costumes to the bonfire," Mom continued. "They were made of animal skins and bones. Some farmers also wore animal heads. This is how the tradition of dressing up got started."

"What about the pumpkins, Mom? How did they become part of Halloween?" Jerry asked.

"The pumpkin part of Halloween started from the story of a man named Jack," Mom said. "People believed that after he died he walked around the earth carrying a lantern.

"So folks would hollow out pumpkins or turnips and put candles in them. Then they set the pumpkins and turnips outside their front gates to scare away the evil spirits who might think Jack was there. That's why they are called Jack-o-lanterns," Mom continued.

"That makes sense," Sarah replied.

"Do you see," Mom asked, "how Halloween centers around evil, scary things? In fact, many costumes picture witches, ghosts, goblins, and other evil creatures that are enemies of God.

"Jesus does not want us to have anything to do with evil," Mom added.* "If we are Jesus' friends, how can we have fun when we look and act like His enemies? Joy comes from being like Jesus."

"If Halloween is so evil, why do so many Christian schools and churches still go trick-or-treating, march in parades, and have Halloween parties?" Jerry asked.

* See Deuteronomy 18:10-13.

"Hundreds of years ago," Mom began, "the rulers of Rome passed a law that everyone had to accept Christianity, the new state religion. Most people became Christians because they had to, not because they wanted to. Instead of giving up their wicked beliefs and the worship of other gods, they added these things to Christianity. Halloween is one example of this.

"When the rulers of Rome tried to stop Halloween parties, the people became angry. They saw nothing wrong with mixing their false beliefs with the worship of Jesus.

"So the Roman rulers moved a Christian holiday, All Saints Day, to November 1st and gave October 31st the name Halloween, which means Holy Evening. Then they told the people to pray for the dead on Halloween, instead of praying to other gods."

"So Halloween became a religious holiday because the Roman leaders changed its name?" Jerry asked.

"Not really," Mom replied. "Halloween was always a religious holiday, but it wasn't a Christian holiday. It still isn't.

"Changing the name of something doesn't change what it is," Mom added. "If I call you Sarah instead of Jerry, that doesn't make you Sarah. It only changes what I call you. So the name, Halloween, doesn't change what is really happening on October 31st. It's just playing 'Let's Make a Deal' with the devil."

"I wouldn't want to do that," Jerry said.

"Me neither," Sarah added.

"So is Halloween still a holy evening?" Jerry asked.

"Not for Christians," Mom answered. "The activities of Halloween lead us to believe that satan and his followers have power over our lives. This is not true. The Bible tells us that Jesus is greater and more powerful than any evil spirit.* Nothing can harm us when we are under His protection."

"Mommy, do you really believe all these things?" Sarah asked.

"Yes, I do, Sarah," Mom replied. "Some people think I'm making a big deal over nothing, but God has placed Daddy and me over you to protect you and to teach you about Jesus.** We are not willing to give satan the tiniest crack to enter your lives and hurt you. It's the joy, peace, and good news of Jesus that we want to plant in your hearts and minds. We cannot allow you to do something we know dishonors Him. That's why we don't permit Halloween in our home.

"The Bible teaches us to do and say everything in the name of Jesus,"*** Mom added. "We certainly can't take part in Halloween in His name. Yet there are many things we can enjoy because Jesus is a Friend who shares love and joy. He wants us to have fun doing good things that bring us laughter, friendship, and peace."

*   See First John 4:4.
**   See Proverbs 22:6.
*** See Colossians 3:17.

"I think I understand a little better now, Mom," Jerry said. "You want us to honor and obey Jesus, not satan."

"That's right, Jerry," Mom answered. "As Christians, we shouldn't allow anything that even looks like evil to be part of our lives."*

"It's not easy to honor Jesus when we can't share in the fun other kids have," Sarah said.

"Remember, children," Mom warned, "what you choose to do for fun must never harm your relationship with Jesus. You cannot grow in your friendship with Him if you do things that dishonor Him.

"Instead of following the example of your friends as they dress up and go trick-or-treating, you need to think of other fun things to do on Halloween night," Mom suggested. "Maybe you two would like to fold socks and do the dishes tonight."

* See First Thessalonians 5:22.

"Come on, Mom! Since when are chores fun?!" asked Jerry.

Mom chuckled and put her arms around Sarah and Jerry. "Think of all the work the children in the Bible did!"

"Yeah!" Sarah agreed as she grinned. "Just think, Jerry, you can do chores for seven years plus another seven years for the privilege of marrying your true love, like Jacob worked for Rachel."*

"Oh yeah?" Jerry objected. "That certainly doesn't sound like fun to me."

"Seriously, children," Mom said, "your dad and I have planned a special family time for this evening. We thought we'd all go out for pizza and a movie."

"That's a great idea, Mom!" Sarah agreed.

Jerry gave his mom a big hug and said, "I love you, Mom. The next time someone asks me why we don't celebrate Halloween, I'll know just what to say."

*   See Genesis 29:9-28.

Suggested Lesson Plan

1. Have the children gather around a wall calendar. (Use small groups around several calendars in the classroom.)

2. Ask the children to look at the holidays represented on the calendar by either words or pictures.

3. Discuss how the children's families celebrate each holiday.

4. Discuss the history of each holiday. (For younger children the teacher should tell something about the origin of each holiday. Older children can work in small groups, with each group researching and reporting on different holidays.)

5. Ask the children: Which holidays are based on events from the Bible? Will what you have learned about the history and origin of the holidays change how you celebrate them? What changes would you make, if any?

The Story Behind the Book

Every year my children were made fun of because they didn't participate in Halloween activities. The answers, "We don't celebrate Halloween because we are Christians," and "Our mother won't let us dress up or go trick-or-treating," didn't stop the teasing. My children needed a resource about the traditions of Halloween the other kids could read and understand.

Five years ago I went into a Christian bookstore looking for a children's book on why Christians shouldn't celebrate Halloween. I was stunned when the sales clerk informed me that, to her knowledge, there were no books for Christian children about Halloween. I was even more shocked when she suggested that I write such a book.

For two years I couldn't stop thinking about writing a book on Halloween. It wasn't that I didn't want to write the book; I just lacked the self-confidence to do it.

You see, as a child, I sat quietly with 52 other children in my class. I pretended to understand what was being taught, but much of the time I did not. I said nothing because I feared being made fun of or being punished.

Therefore, I didn't learn—even though my mother tried to help me with homework. I was in third grade before I learned to read, and in sixth grade before I learned to tell time. Thus, I feared what the reaction of my family would be if I told them I was writing a book: "Linda's writing a book. When did she learn to read?"

Three years after I'd gone to the bookstore looking for a book about Halloween for Christian children, I awoke with the words of this book going over and over in my head. When I questioned the Lord what to do with them, His answer was clear: "Get to work."

That night I began to write this book. It wasn't until Halloween of that year, as my friend Susan and I discussed our yearly struggle with this holiday, that I told anyone what I had done. September of the following year I received a call from Susan, who was then working with a children's street ministry. She asked me to pray about finishing my book so she could give it to the children before Halloween.

I did pray about this book, and God answered my prayer. One week before Halloween, we printed and distributed more than 700 copies in our small area alone!

God has big dreams for all children. He uses ordinary people to do His extraordinary work. That's why, in spite of my struggles, I could not escape the certainty that God had chosen me to write a book for Christian children about Halloween.

The Bible promises that all will be well for those who listen for God's voice and obey Him. My prayer is that all children, no matter what difficulties they struggle with, will be encouraged by this story to see that with God all things are possible.

Linda Hacon Winwood

The Mommy Why? Series

**MOMMY, WHY DON'T WE
CELEBRATE HALLOWEEN?**
by Linda Hacon Winwood.
TPB-24p. ISBN 1-56043-823-1
Retail $2.99 (8" X 9")

**MOMMY, WAS SANTA CLAUS
BORN ON CHRISTMAS TOO?**
by Barbara Knoll.
TPB-24p. ISBN 1-56043-158-X
Retail $2.99 (8" X 9")

**MOMMY, WHY DID JESUS
HAVE TO DIE?**
by Dian Layton.
TPB-24p. ISBN 1-56043-146-6
Retail $2.99 (8" X 9")

**MOMMY, ARE YOU AFRAID
OF MONSTERS?**
by Barbara Knoll.
TPB-24p. ISBN 1-56043-149-0
Retail $2.99 (8" X 9")

**MOMMY, WHY CAN'T I
WATCH THAT TV SHOW?**
by Dian Layton.
TPB-24p. ISBN 1-56043-148-2
Retail $2.99 (8" X 9")

**DADDY, DOES GOD
TAKE A VACATION?**
by Galen C. Burkholder.
TPB-24p. ISBN 1-56043-153-9
Retail $2.99 (8" X 9")

**MOMMY, IS GOD AS
STRONG AS DADDY?**
by Barbara Knoll.
TPB-24p. ISBN 1-56043-150-4
Retail $2.99 (8" X 9")

**MOMMY, WHY ARE PEOPLE
DIFFERENT COLORS?**
by Barbara Knoll.
TPB-24p. ISBN 1-56043-156-3
Retail $2.99 (8" X 9")

**Internet:
http://www.reapernet.com**

HINDS' FEET ON HIGH PLACES
(Illustrated Version)
by Hannah Hurnard.
This illustrated version of the classic tale of "Much-Afraid" will take your children on a wonder-filled journey of excitement and joy through dangerous forests and up steep cliffs to the very home of the "Shepherd." It will draw them closer to our Savior with every word and colorful illustration!
HB-128p. ISBN 1-56043-111-3
(7" X 9") Retail $14.99

THE AMAZING LAMB OF GOD
by Dr. Richard E. Eby.
This unique collection of stories from the author's childhood has been specially prepared to teach biblical principles for Kingdom living. This creative book offers a charming look at close family relationships that provide meaningful context for learning spiritual lessons.
TPB-182p. ISBN 1-56043-803-7
Retail $8.99

THE BATTLE FOR THE SEED
by Dr. Patricia Morgan.
The dilemma facing young people today is a major concern for all parents. This important book of the 90's shows God's way to change the condition of the young and advance God's purpose for every nation into the next century.
TPB-112p. ISBN 1-56043-099-0
Retail $8.99

SOLDIERS WITH LITTLE FEET
by Dian Layton.
Every time God pours out His Spirit, the adult generation moves on without its children. Dian pleads with the Church to bring the children into the fullness of God with them and offers practical guidelines for doing so.
TPB-182p. ISBN 0-914903-86-1
Retail $7.99

PERFECTED PRAISE
by Richard Malm.
Praise is perfected in the hearts of children. In this book, the author addresses the difficult task of leading children to encounter Jesus Himself through praise and worship. This title will challenge those who desire to lead their children toward fellowship with Christ.
TPB-96p. ISBN 0-914903-62-4
Retail $6.99

TELL ME AGAIN
by Dr. Patricia Morgan.
Tell Me Again is one woman's call to hear the cry of the hurting, broken children of the nations. An educational psychologist, a professor, and a mother, Dr. Patricia Morgan combines her culture, her beliefs, and her passion to issue a ringing challenge in this unique collection of writings. This book will stir your heart like nothing else can!
TPB-144p. ISBN 1-56043-180-6
(6" X 9") Retail $10.99